Big Bird Gets Lost

By Patricia Thackray
Illustrated by Carol Nicklaus

A SESAME STREET/GOLDEN PRESS BOOK
Published by Western Publishing Company, Inc.,
in conjunction with Children's Television Workshop.

Featuring Jim Henson's Sesame Street Muppets

One morning, Big Bird hurried into Mr. Hooper's store on Sesame Street. "Hi, Mr. Blooper! Boy, am I glad to find you here! I'd like a sack of your best birdseed, please."

"Sorry, Big Bird," said Mr. Hooper, "I'm all sold out."

Big Bird's feathers nearly stood on end.

"But you can't be out of birdseed!" he wailed. "Not today!"

"What's so important about today?" asked Mr. Hooper.

"My old nest wore out, so I built a new one, and I'm giving a nest-warming party for everybody on Sesame Street . . ."

"I see . . ." said Mr. Hooper.

"Uh-oh. He's sure to get lost. I'd better tag along."

"I need lots and lots of birdseed *now*," explained Big Bird, "so I can make a . . . oops! I almost gave away my surprise."

"Don't worry, Big Bird," said Mr. Hooper. "I'm expecting a delivery of birdseed this afternoon."

"But I *can't wait*!" cried Big Bird.

"Well, in that case, Big Bird, try the A & B grocery store."

"That's a great idea," said Big Bird. "I'll go right now. 'Bye, Mr. Gooper!"

"The name's Hooper, Big Bird, but wait a minute. Do you know how to get to the A & B? I'll tell you. Turn right at the corner and go one block straight ahead. Turn left and walk two blocks. Turn right and walk three more blocks."

"Oh, that's a snap!" said Big Bird. "Easy as birdseed pie!"

"Well, don't get lost, Big Bird," warned Mr. Hooper.

"Lost? Me, lost? Never! See you at my party. Five o'clock at my new nest. 'Bye, Mr. Dooper!"

"Dee-dum-dee-dum-dee-dum. Two blocks left and three blocks right," sang Big Bird as he passed the park.

Suddenly he heard tinkly music and sniffed a delicious smell that wafted by his beak.

"Ohhh, something smells wonderful," said Big Bird—and he headed into the park.

"Well, look at that!" said Big Bird. "A merry-go-round and a pizza stand!"

Big Bird bought a slice of pizza and waited in line for a ride on the merry-go-round.

I love pizza, don't you? You can smell this piece if you scratch and sniff it.

When it was his turn, Big Bird rode around and around, singing at the top of his lungs, "Oh, I'm a happy, happy yellow bird!"

"Why are you so happy, Big Bird?" asked Sweetina, who was riding next to him.

"Because I'm having a nest-warming party tonight and everybody's invited. Five o'clock sharp!"

"Oh, dear," thought Big Bird, "I'm having such a terrific ride that I almost forgot about the birdseed! See you later, everybody," he said, as he lurched off the merry-go-round and back down the path.

"Hey, look out, you dizzy bird!" yelled the pizza vendor.

"Now, where was that store? Let's see . . . three blocks to the right and five blocks to the left . . .?"

Uh...one block right and four blocks left?

Big Bird stumbled out of the park, his head still spinning.
He staggered right into the first store he saw—Kelly's Deli.
Next to the counter was a big wooden barrel.

"Oh, lucky me! A whole big barrel of birdseed!" exclaimed
Big Bird, and he stuck his head in to look.

But it wasn't birdseed! Kelly, the deli owner, looked at the strange yellow bird with the pickle on his beak and said, "You want me to wrap that pickle or will you eat it here?"

"Mmuff, I meed bddsd . . ." said Big Bird.

Kelly pulled off the pickle. "How's that again?"

"I need birdseed," said Big Bird.

"In a deli?" asked Kelly. "You've come to the wrong place. You can't buy birdseed in a delicatessen. Why don't you try the A & B grocery store? You can't miss it."

Big Bird invited Kelly to his party and left the deli. Directly across the street was a big old stone building.

"Wow!" thought Big Bird as he climbed up the steps of the building. "Kelly was right. You sure can't miss it. What a big grocery store!"

"Hi there!" he called to the librarian. "Is this the A & B?"

"Kindly lower your voice," said the librarian. "May I help you?" he whispered.

"Sure. I'm looking for birdseed," Big Bird whispered back.

"*Birdseed*? I've never heard of it. Who wrote it?" asked the librarian. "I'll have to look it up in my card catalog."

Big Bird waited anxiously while the librarian searched
through all the B's.

"I'm sorry," he said, "but we have nothing under that title."

"What? No birdseed?" Big Bird shouted. "But I came all
the way here to buy some!"

"Shhh!" said the people at the tables, looking up from their
books and magazines.

"This is a library, not a seed store!" the librarian whispered
loudly. "Try the A & B grocery store. You can't miss it!"

"Oh," said Big Bird. "Excuse me." And he tiptoed away.

Right next door to the library was a plant store with some brightly colored seed packets displayed on an outdoor rack. As soon as he spotted it, Big Bird was sure that he had found the right place at last.

"Sully says, 'Whadjuh say?'" said Biff.

"I need birdseed fast!" said Big Bird.

"Sully says, 'Try the A & B grocery store!'" said Biff.

"I *am* trying," said Big Bird, "but where *is* it?"

"Sully says, 'Go two blocks . . .'" began Biff. Just then, Sully started up on the jackhammer.

Poor Big Bird. He couldn't hear a word!

What a racket!

"Oh, I'm never going to find the A & B," moaned Big Bird. "And it's getting so late. Hey, wait a minute! I bet Mr. Cooper has gotten his birdseed delivery by now. That's it! *I'll go back to Sesame Street!*"

He took one step to the right. He took two steps to the left. He turned around in a circle.

"Which way *is* Sesame Street?" he cried. "Oh, dear! I'm lost!"

Then Big Bird ran into the nearest phone booth, dropped a dime in the slot, and dialed "O" for operator.

"Hello, operator, this is Big Bird. I'd like to call Mr. Gooper's store on Sesame Street."

"One moment, please," said the operator. Big Bird waited impatiently.

"I'm sorry," said the operator, "but we have no Mr. Gooper's store listed at that address."

"No Mr. . . . but that's impossible! I was just there this morning. Oh, dear, now what can I do?"

Big Bird came out of the phone booth feeling more lost than ever. "I guess I'll have to ask somebody how to get home," he said. He paused to look in the window of a hair salon.

"Maybe someone in here can help," he said, and went inside.

"Uh, excuse me," he said to a hairdresser. "Can you tell me how to get . . ."

"A shampoo and blow dry?" asked the hairdresser. "Of course. Right this way."

"Thank you, but I don't have time right now," Big Bird said. But before he knew what was happening, he was sitting in a barber chair with his head in a sink of warm, sudsy water.

"Oh, this feels nice," he said. "Maybe I'll just rest here a minute or two."

And while Big Bird was napping, a hairdresser gave him a special strawberry shampoo!

Feeling like a new bird after his nap and shampoo, Big Bird hurried out into the sunshine to find his way home. The very first thing he saw was a sign that read, "Madame Zornow: All Questions Answered."

"Goody!" he said. "That's just what I need—an answer to my question."

"Sit down, big bird," commanded Madame Zornow, "and I will read your palm feathers."

"Gee, how did you know my name?" asked Big Bird.

"Madame Zornow knows all," she answered, looking at his palm feathers. "I see much birdseed in your future . . ."

"Oh, that's really terrific, but I need birdseed right *now*!"

". . . and many friends," she continued.

"Yes," said Big Bird excitedly. "I'm looking for my friend Mr. Hooper."

"I will look into my crystal ball," said Madame Zornow.

We'll never get anywhere this way.

Madame Zornow lit some incense and waved her hands over the crystal ball. "I see your friend Mr. Hooper," she said. "He is far, far away."

"No he isn't," answered Big Bird. "He's always in his store on Sesame Street."

"Right," said Madame Zornow. "On faraway Sesame Street."

"Sesame Street isn't far away," said Big Bird, "it's right around *here* somewhere." Big Bird stood up. "*You* can't tell me how to get to Sesame Street. I'll have to find it myself."

Big Bird went running down the street, calling for Mr. Hooper. He ran until he couldn't run any more. Finally, he sat down, exhausted, on the curb.

"Oh dear, oh my! I'll never find my way home, and I'll be the only one who doesn't come to my party. And what about the surprise I was going to make?"

Suddenly Big Bird heard a voice behind him calling, "Big Bird!" He turned around and saw Mr. Hooper coming toward him. And then he saw Ernie and Bert and Grover and Oscar. And then he saw his very own new nest.

Big Bird had found his way back to Sesame Street without even knowing it!

"I got my birdseed delivery," said Mr. Hooper, "and I was just coming to look for you. I was afraid you were lost."

"Me, lost?" said Big Bird. "Don't be silly, Mr. Flooper."

So Big Bird got his birdseed at Mr. Hooper's store after all.
And he still had time to run home and prepare his surprise.
At five o'clock everyone showed up for the nest-warming,
and Big Bird brought out his surprise—a giant birdseed pie!